FOOTBALL MAD 2
OFFSIDE!

On the pitch, the compliments were coming in thick and fast as Gary was surrounded by his team-mates. "Great shot, mate!" "Fantastic kick, Gary!" "Real magic!"

"I couldn't have done it without Leigh's pass," said Gary generously. "It was spot on."

"Yeah," said Wesley, patting Leigh on the back. "It was a brilliant pass."

Leigh ducked his head. "Thanks," he mumbled. He turned away. He looked uneasy.

As far as Leigh Parker was concerned, getting through to the final was the easy bit. For him, the really hard stuff was just about to begin.

If you enjoyed **Football Mad II**, check out St Botolph's first great cup run in **Football Mad**, also by Paul Stewart. *It's a scorcher!*

Ace football writer Rob Childs brings you cracking soccer adventure across space and time! Join the **Time Rangers** for:

1. A Shot in the Dark
2. A Blast from the Past
3. A Race Against Time
4. A Ghost of a Chance
5. A Toss of the Coin
6. A Sting in the Tale

More great titles in the Hippo Sport series:

Henry's Boots
Anthony Lishak

Hopeless Haines and the No-Hopers
Martin Hodgson

The Winning Touch
David Hill

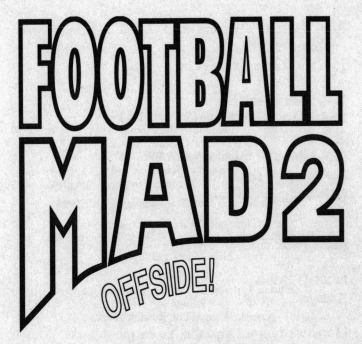

FOOTBALL MAD 2

OFFSIDE!

Paul Stewart

Hippo

Scholastic Children's Books,
Commonwealth House,
1-19 New Oxford Street,
London WC1A 1NU, UK
A division of Scholastic Ltd
London ~ New York ~ Toronto ~ Sydney ~ Auckland

First published in the UK by Scholastic Ltd, 1998

Copyright © Paul Stewart, 1998
Inside illustrations copyright © David Kearney, 1998

ISBN 0 590 11272 4

Typeset by
Cambrian Typesetters, Frimley, Camberley, Surrey
Printed by
Cox & Wyman Ltd, Reading, Berks

2 4 6 8 10 9 7 5 3 1

for Joseph, Ciaran
and Aidan

Chapter 1

Gary Connell crossed his fingers for good luck. He was feeling nervous. The score was one-all. It had been one-all since half-time and, with less than five minutes of play remaining, the atmosphere was reaching fever pitch. Whichever team scored next would win the match and go through to the final of the Mereside Borough Junior Cup. And with the opposition's main striker bearing down upon the St Botolph's goal, things were looking decidedly dangerous.

"Come on, Danny, you can do it," Gary muttered encouragingly.

At the other end of the field, Danny Thompson, the goalie, was bouncing from foot to foot. The opposition's number 9 had already scored once. Now he had broken through the St Botolph's defence again, and it was all down to Danny to make sure that Hume Juniors didn't snatch victory in the closing minutes of the game.

Keeping his eye on the ball, Danny dashed towards the advancing forward to cut the angle of the open goal and, he hoped, force their striker into hurrying the shot and messing it up.

The number 9 got closer. He slowed down, he glanced up at the goal and – BOOF – he struck the ball hard and low with his left foot.

Danny dived, arms outstretched. The ball clipped his fingers – but kept on going. Danny groaned. He rolled over and looked up, fully expecting to see the ball hurtling into the back of the net.

But no! Although he'd hardly touched it, Danny had managed to deflect the ball. It struck the far-side post and dropped down.

But the danger was not yet over. The ball was still in play and their number 9 was sprinting towards it to finish the job off.

Danny scrambled desperately to his feet, raced back and hurled himself down at the ball. The attacker went to shoot. Danny landed heavily at his feet, seized the ball and curled himself around it. He felt a boot whistling harmlessly past his ear. A cheer and a groan echoed round the rows of supporters. He'd done it!

Up at the other end, Gary was ecstatic. The game wasn't over yet – far from it. St Botolph's had possession of the ball. If they were quick, and did exactly what they had practised so many times at training sessions, they could still win.

As Danny climbed to his feet, Gary glanced over his shoulder to check he was still being marked. He was. Their number 6 had been stuck to him like a leech for the whole match. Gary trotted back towards the centre line, drawing the Hume defender with him.

All round him, the St Botolph's supporters were urging them on to victory. "Come on, you Paint Boys!" they roared, over and over.

Gary grinned. This was the first season in the cup's history that local companies had been allowed to sponsor the individual teams. St Botolph's – who were being sponsored by Pringle's Paint – were playing in a bright red strip with the company's logo emblazoned across the front of their shirts. Although the nickname was inevitable, Gary still hadn't got used to hearing it being chanted.

"Yeah, come on now, Paint Boys," he said to himself. He looked round the pitch. "Before they get back into position."

Still reeling from the disappointment of the missed goal, Hume Juniors were all over the place. Danny took advantage of the situation. He bounced the ball quickly – once, twice – and rolled the ball out to Maurice Meacham. Maurice ran for a couple of metres before punting it on to Wesley Hunter who, without stopping, chipped it over to the left wing, where Leigh Parker was waiting, unmarked.

Gary watched the sequence of moves with growing excitement. "Come on, come on," he whispered urgently.

Mr Talbot, their football coach, had spent a long time over the previous term concentrating on the finer points of the offside rule. "Offside," as he was fond of saying, "is being in the right place at the wrong time. What you've got to do is be there at the right time."

So far, the set piece was working like a dream. Now it was up to Gary to make sure that the manoeuvre resulted in a goal.

He could no longer hear the crowd. Concentrating one hundred per cent on the ball, it was as though the entire world had fallen silent. He had to be fast. He had to be accurate. He had to time his run to perfection. He watched Leigh's every move as he dribbled the ball round one of their midfield players, steadied up – and kicked. The ball soared into the air and up the field in a long, curving arc.

The moment the ball left Leigh's boot, Gary was away. Finally shaking off his leech-like marker, he sprinted up towards the opposition goal to receive the ball as it floated back down to earth.

The spectators could see what was happening. Some roared with approval. Others pleaded for "offside". But the linesman's flag remained down. Having drawn the Hume defender forward, Gary had been careful to keep just in front of him when the ball was kicked. Now he was behind him, on his own, and still running. The ball dropped at his feet. He trapped it, spun round and tapped it forwards. There was only the goalie between him and victory.

"Easy now," he told himself. The goalie was running towards him. "Don't rush it. Take your time." Behind him, he could hear the opposition defence getting closer and closer. "Now!"

He chipped the ball, deftly but firmly, up into the air. The goalie leaped up, but the ball flew past his flailing arms and on towards the net. Gary froze. The spectators fell still. Was it going to be a goal, or was the ball travelling too far over to the left?

"YEAH!" A roar of jubilation went up from the St Botolph's supporters.

It *was* a goal. A perfect goal, with the ball slamming into the corner of the net. Gary dropped to his knees, fists clenched. The goalie – sprawled out across the muddy goal-mouth – stared forlornly down at the ground. He'd never stood a chance.

Then the ref blew the whistle for the end of play, and the crowd roared even louder. Two-one! They'd done it. St Botolph's were through to the final of the Mereside Borough Junior Cup for the second year running. Last year they'd won it. Now they had the chance to make it a double.

On the pitch, the compliments were coming in thick and fast as Gary was surrounded by his team-mates. "Great shot, mate!" "Fantastic kick, Gary!" "Real magic!"

"I couldn't have done it without Leigh's pass," said Gary generously. "It was spot on."

"Yeah," said Wesley, patting Leigh on the back. "It was a brilliant pass."

Leigh ducked his head. "Thanks," he mumbled. He turned away. He looked uneasy.

As far as Leigh Parker was concerned, getting through to the final was the easy bit. For him, the really hard stuff was just about to begin.

Chapter 2

Craig Taggart had not been playing in the game. With number 12 on his back, he had spent the entire match watching from the reserves' bench. He was, of course, overjoyed that his team had made it through to the final, and was cheering along with everyone else – but inside Craig felt sick to his stomach that he hadn't been allowed to help them get there.

He stared miserably at Leigh. It was because of him that Craig had lost his place in the team.

* * *

Leigh Parker had joined the class at the beginning of the spring term. It's never easy changing schools in the middle of the year but Leigh was better equipped than most. For a start, he was big for his age and, with his crew cut and the scar which cut through his left eyebrow, he did not look like the kind of boy you'd want to mess with. More importantly, he was passionate about football.

Craig, Gary and Danny – who shared the same passion – had immediately taken him under their wing. On that first day, they let him join their lunchtime Fantasy Football League, introduced him to the rest of the team and, when school was over, they invited him to join them up the rec for a kick-about. They played Corner and Three-'n-in.

It was soon clear that Leigh was as good at playing as he was knowledgeable about international players. He tackled hard, he headed accurately and his footwork was a dream.

"You should try out for a place in the team," Gary had said enthusiastically.

"Yeah," Danny had agreed. "Then we can finally get rid of Luke Edwards."

They'd all laughed. But even then, Craig remembered, he had felt uneasy. Leigh Parker played left midfield, which was where he, Craig, liked to be. What if it wasn't Luke Edwards who was dropped from the team, but him?

Later that week, after the football trials, Mr Talbot stood in the changing room saying that a place would have to be found in the team for "this excellent new talent". Although Gary and Danny assured him he was imagining it, Craig felt sure Mr Talbot was looking at him at the time. Sure enough, the following week, Craig was pulled in the second half of the match and Leigh Parker was sent on in his place. He set up two goals, scored one of his own – and gained a permanent place in the team.

Naturally, Craig had been gutted. Not only had he been dropped from the school team, but he felt as if he was losing his two best friends. He, Gary Connell and Danny Thompson went back a long way. They'd known each other since the infants, and had played football up the rec together for more than seven years. With the arrival of Leigh Parker, all this abruptly changed.

The threesome became a foursome. And though no one actually *said* anything, the fact remained that three of them were in the team and one of them wasn't. It made a difference.

The worst of it was, Craig wasn't sure he even *liked* Leigh. He was cocky and loud. He was always showing off, always cracking stupid jokes. Unfortunately, no one else saw him the same way. To Danny, Gary and everyone else, he was confident, interesting – and *very* good at football.

In the old days, Craig would have talked to Danny and Gary about Leigh, to get it off his chest. Now, that was no longer possible. He had to keep his opinion of Leigh Parker to himself. After all, he knew what would happen if he did say anything. The others would accuse him of sour grapes.

As he continued to watch his rival, Craig had to admit that now, at least, Leigh was looking anything but cocky. Head down, he was shuffling about awkwardly as the others slapped him on the back. To anyone who didn't know him, he seemed like a modest boy who was embarrassed by all the attention he was getting.

But Craig did know him. He knew him only too well. Normally, Leigh would have been more than happy to bathe in the glory of setting up the winning goal. So why wasn't he acting normally now?

Craig shrugged. "Who cares?" he told himself. The Paint Boys were through to the final, and that was what mattered. And with that thought, he raced on to the pitch to congratulate Danny, Gary and the rest of the team on a fantastic victory.

As they were all making their way back to the changing rooms, Craig found himself walking next to his rival. "Great pass, Leigh," he said, loud enough for the others to hear. He never wanted *anyone* to guess just how jealous he was.

Leigh looked round and smiled. "Thanks," he said.

"So," said Craig. "Next week, the final."

At the sound of the word, Leigh winced. The smile disappeared from his face.

"What is it?" said Craig.

"Nothing," said Leigh. He turned away and quickened his pace. Craig could only stand and watch as he strode off, wondering what he had said to make Leigh act so strangely.

Chapter 3

Unlike all the other qualifying matches, which had been played on Wednesdays, the final of the Mereside Cup was to take place on a Saturday. This gave the Paint Boys ten days to tighten up their game. Every afternoon after school, Mr Talbot arranged for a training session, and every evening after that, Danny, Gary, Craig and Leigh went up to the rec to concentrate on their passing and shooting.

It was on the first Friday, after two hours of Corner, Three-'n-in and a new game they'd devised called Offside, when Craig announced that he had something important to say.

"It's my birthday on Sunday…" he told them.

Leigh laughed. "Fishing for presents, eh?"

Craig ignored him. "…and Mum and Dad are giving me some money to spend with three friends up at Leisureland. So," he said, "can you all make it?"

"You bet," said Danny.

"Certainly can," said Gary. "Can we go bowling?"

"Yep," said Craig. "I thought swimming first, then bowling, then burger, chips and a shake in the café and then…" He paused dramatically, and when he spoke again it was in a deep, spooky voice. "*Brainblaster III*."

"Fantastic!" Danny and Gary said together.

Craig turned to Leigh, who still

hadn't said anything. "Well?" he asked.

Leigh looked up, but wouldn't meet Craig's gaze. "I ... I don't think I can," he said.

Craig didn't try to persuade him. He'd only asked him along in the first place because it would have been too awkward *not* to ask him. To tell the truth, he was relieved that, for his birthday treat at least, it would just be him and his two best and oldest friends.

"What'll you be doing, then?" Gary asked Leigh.

"Oh, this and that," he replied vaguely. "There's someone I've got to see." He looked thoughtful for a moment. His brow furrowed with worry. "And I can't get out of it."

Gary and Danny glanced at one another. They, like Craig, could see that Leigh was not his usual self.

"Oh well, never mind, mate," said Gary. "It's *my* birthday next month. We'll all do something together then."

Leigh nodded miserably. "Maybe," he said. "If..." He stopped.

"What?" said Gary.

"Nothing!" He turned to Craig. "So what time do the fun and games get started?" he said.

"Ten o'clock," said Craig. "At the main entrance."

"And you're going swimming first, right?" said Leigh.

"Yeah, why?" He paused. "If you've got time, you could meet us there and then shoot off afterwards."

Leigh shook his head. "No, I..." He swallowed. "I just wondered. Anyway," he said, smiling weakly, "I'd better be off. See ya." And with that he abruptly turned away, and set off towards the park gates.

Gary, Danny and Craig watched him

go. "What was all that about?" said Danny finally.

"Search me," said Gary.

"He's been acting odd since Wednesday," said Craig. "Didn't you see his face at the end of the match?"

Gary and Danny shook their heads. They'd been too overjoyed at winning the semi-final to notice anything!

Gary shrugged. "It's probably just pre-match nerves."

"That's what I thought," said Craig. "It's just that, well... I mean, Leigh doesn't seem like the type to get nervous before a game, does he?"

"S'pose not," Gary agreed. "Has he said anything to you, Danny?"

"No," said Danny. "P'raps he's got problems at home."

"P'raps," said Craig.

"Well, whatever it is," said Gary, "I just hope it doesn't spoil his game on the big day."

Craig nodded, but remained silent. If

there *was* something the matter with Leigh, then maybe – just maybe – he would get to play after all.

* * *

The Sunday of Craig's birthday was cold and overcast, but since the Leisureland Complex was all under cover, it didn't matter. Craig and Danny cycled into town together. They arrived at the Complex to find Gary already waiting for them.

"Hiya," they greeted one another.

"No sign of Leigh, then?" said Danny.

"No," said Gary. "I didn't think he'd come."

"Shame," Craig lied, hoping the others hadn't noticed how relieved he was.

"Happy birthday, mate," said Gary. "Here's your present."

"Thanks," said Craig. He tore off the wrapping paper. It was a book. "*The*

Making of Brainblaster III," Craig read and began flicking through pages of film stills, step-by-step stunts and gory special effects. "It's fantastic!" he said. "Thanks a lot."

"What did you get him?" Gary asked Danny.

"Underwater goggles," he said.

"What, Dynamo goggles?" said Gary. Danny nodded. Gary turned to Craig. "Let's have a look."

Craig pulled the new goggles from his sports bag and handed them over. They were light but solid, with non-mist glass and special side valves that changed according to the pressure as you dived deeper. They came with a lifetime guarantee.

Gary was impressed. "Wow!" he said. "Can I have a go with them?"

Craig laughed. "Long as you don't lose them." Gary was notoriously bad at returning things he'd borrowed.

"Actually," Craig added, "slight change of plan. They don't start up the wave-machine till eleven, so I thought we'd go bowling first. Is that OK?"

Gary and Danny nodded. "Fine by me," said Gary.

"Come on, then," said Craig. "Let's go in."

As he walked through the swing doors into the bowling hall, Craig grinned. He loved everything about ten-pin bowling – the soft leather shoes he had to wear, the rumble of the heavy balls as they hurtled down the alleys, the clatter of the skittles scattering this way and that. What was more, he was good at it.

Usually.

Perhaps he was overexcited because it was his birthday. Perhaps he couldn't keep his mind off the film they were going to see later. Whatever, that

Sunday morning he played hopelessly. While Danny and Gary battled it out for the lead, Craig was trailing badly.

It was only on his seventh go that the electronic scoreboard began to register a comeback. He got a spare, followed by a succession of strikes. First he caught up, then he equalized with Danny, who was just ahead of Gary, and finally he won.

"Well done, Craigy-boy," said Danny, as they changed back into their trainers.

"Course, we only let you win because it's your birthday," said Gary.

Craig laughed and punched him on the arm.

Bowling over, their next stop was the swimming-pool. There, they spent the next hour whooping and screaming as they hurtled down the water chutes and body-surfed the waves.

The goggles were fantastic, too. You

could see perfectly underwater, and not a drop of water got in. Craig found a pound coin on the bottom of the deep end.

"My lucky day!" he announced, as he emerged triumphantly from the water, arm up-stretched.

As if on cue, both Gary and Danny immediately lunged for it. Craig tried his best to make a getaway, but it was hopeless. As Gary pushed his head under, Danny grabbed his legs. Ducking and being ducked, it was an instant bundle as the three boys kicked, squirmed and thrashed about. The pool attendant was on them like a shot.

"Oy! You lot!" he bellowed. "OUT! Go and get changed, now!"

They all protested, of course. You have to, don't you? But none of them really minded. They were all getting tired; they were all extremely hungry.

Craig sat in his changing cubicle staring down at the tiled floor. He knew he ought to be feeling happier than he was. After all, it was his birthday, he was out with his friends, the morning had been great and the afternoon promised to be even better. And yet, despite all this, Craig could not forget that the final of the Mereside Borough Junior Cup was in six days' time – and he wouldn't be playing. It was like a big, black cloud hanging over him.

"Are you ready, Craig?" he heard Danny and Gary asking from outside.

"Not yet," he said. He wasn't even dry yet. 'I'll meet you up in the Burger Bar."

"OK," said Danny.

"But don't be long," Gary added. "I'm starving!"

As their footsteps faded away, Craig climbed to his feet, towelled himself down and began getting dressed. I should be looking forward to the final, he thought miserably. I should be excited. He sighed. "Damn Leigh Parker!" he muttered. "I wish he'd never come to St Botolph's."

Just then, the cubicle doors on either side of him slammed shut. The loud noise brought Craig back from his thoughts with a jolt.

It was clear that the two people were together. They talked across Craig's cubicle to one another. Craig froze. One of the voices was deep and rough. He didn't recognize it. But the other voice – younger, higher and sounding slightly uneasy – was all too familiar.

Craig was in no doubt. It was Leigh Parker.

Chapter 4

Craig's first thought was to announce himself, but something stopped him. Instead, he listened in on their conversation – not that it made much sense.

"So, Leigh," called the older boy. "You made it through to the final, then?"

"Yeah," said Leigh.

There was a pause, then the older boy said. "Which means you'll be playing Mickelham Mill."

"Yeah."

There was another pause.

"And you won't forget what we agreed?"

"N-no," Leigh stammered. He snorted and added under his breath. "How could I?"

Craig heard the older boy laugh unpleasantly. "How *are* the roller-blades, by the way?"

"Fine," said Leigh.

"And the wrist and elbow guards? And the knee pads? They're OK too, are they?"

Leigh sighed. "Yeah," he said.

"Good," said the other boy. "This means a lot to me, you know."

"I know," said Leigh miserably.

"Long as we understand each other, mate," he went on. "After all, we wouldn't want your mum to find out what you've been up to, would we?"

Leigh remained silent.

Craig's fingers trembled as he did up the laces of his trainers. It sounded as if

Leigh was being bullied by the other boy – blackmailed, even. But why? And what *had* Leigh done that he wouldn't want his mum to hear about?

Dressed at last, Craig stuffed his towel, trunks and goggles inside his holdall and slid the bolt quietly across the door. He wanted to slip away unnoticed so that he could tell Gary and Danny what he had overheard. Tentatively, he pulled the door open and stepped out into the corridor.

Unfortunately, at exactly the same moment, the two adjacent doors burst open. Before Craig could duck back into his cubicle, Leigh and an older boy of fifteen or sixteen, both dressed in trunks, appeared on either side of him.

On seeing Craig, Leigh turned beetroot red, blushing all the way down from his cheeks to his chest. "H-hiya," he said guiltily.

Craig nodded back.

"Friend of yours, eh?" said the older boy. He was big and stocky, with an earring, a tattoo on his upper arm and a shaved head. He looked hard. He looked mean.

"Yeah. This is Craig. He's in my class," said Leigh. "And this is Billy. He's my ... my cousin."

Billy stared at Craig without smiling. "All right, Craig?" he said.

Craig nodded again. He turned to Leigh. "I'll catch you later," he said. "The others are waiting for me upstairs."

He walked to the end of the tiled corridor, turned left at the lockers – and paused. Billy and Leigh were talking again.

"Is he in the team?" Billy was asking.

"First reserve," said Leigh.

Craig scowled, and was about to walk away when Leigh said something else – not to Billy, but muttered angrily under his breath. It *sounded* like, "Offside."

Offside? Craig wondered, and shrugged. I must have misheard him.

Of course, Craig intended telling Danny and Gary all about who he'd met in the changing rooms the moment he saw them. But when he got to the Burger Bar, Gary immediately started moaning on about how hungry he was, and by the time they'd loaded up their trays and found somewhere to sit, they were deep in conversation about which film was better, *Brainblaster I* or *II*.

It was only later, when they were cycling home after the film – which they all agreed was the best so far – that Craig remembered his strange encounter.

The others listened in silence, pedalling slower and slower, as Craig told them everything that had happened, everything that had been said. He was disappointed by their reaction.

"Is that all?" said Gary.

"Not quite," said Craig. "Just as I was leaving I heard Leigh saying something odd."

"What?" asked Danny.

"Offside!" said Craig. "And what does *offside* mean to you?"

"Being in the right place at the wrong time," Danny and Gary chorused. Mr Talbot would have been proud of them.

Gary turned and looked at Craig. "So he said 'offside'. So what?"

"Don't you see?" said Craig. "He must have been talking about me. I was in the swimming-baths at the wrong time. I overheard what he and his cousin were saying. And he didn't like it. That's why he went so red." He paused. "Whatever it is he's up to, it must affect us."

There was a silence. Craig noticed Gary and Danny glancing at one another. Finally Danny spoke.

"Look, Craig," he said. "I'm really sorry you're not in the team, mate, but..."

"If it hadn't been for Leigh, we wouldn't have beaten Hume in the first place," Gary added.

Craig looked away. He'd blown it. His two best friends now thought he was just being spiteful. Because he was jealous. He could see it in the expressions on their faces. They thought that he was reading too much into a harmless conversation – or worse, that he'd made up the whole story.

Somehow, he would have to prove that he was right and they were wrong. If they were ever to be really close friends again, it was the only way.

Chapter 5

The day of the cup final came all too quickly for Craig. He'd tried all week to find out what was worrying Leigh, but even Tracy and Toyah – who generally knew everything about everybody – had no idea what the problem might be. And by the time Saturday arrived, he was still no closer to the truth.

Kick-off was set for two o'clock. At half-past one the two teams were in the changing rooms getting ready. Every player had received a brand-new kit for the final – it was all part of the sponsorship deal. St Botolph's were in their bright red Paint Boys strip. Mickelham Mill, who were advertising Varley's Varnish, were in green.

Pringle's Paint and Varley's Varnish. It was pure chance that the town's two manufacturing rivals were facing one another in the final. The coincidence was not lost on the boys. It made the natural rivalry between the two teams all the sharper.

"We are the Paint Boys! We are the Paint Boys!" St Botolph's chanted. While, on the other side of the changing room wall, the Mickelham Mill team tried to drown them out by singing *Var-nish* over and over, to the tune of Amazing Grace. By the time the two teams trotted out on to the pitch, the atmosphere was charged.

A rousing cheer greeted the boys as they appeared. Being a Saturday, there were far more spectators than usual. It was a warm, breezy afternoon, and everyone was looking forward to an excellent game.

Craig made his way to the substitutes' bench. He had been disappointed – though not surprised – when he heard the team being announced the previous afternoon. Once again, he was first reserve. All he could do was hope that Mr Talbot would put him on at some point in the match.

St Botolph's won the toss and, when the referee blew his whistle, kicked off. Craig sat forward, chewing his nails, watching his team intently – and thinking back to the good old days when he would have been out there playing with them.

As the game got underway, Craig found himself getting more and more irritated by the way Leigh was playing. It was as though he wasn't trying. He was slow, he tackled too softly, and all too often his sloppy passes went straight to the opposition.

"For Pete's sake, get a grip!" Craig yelled. Not playing was bad enough – watching his team being beaten was unbearable.

On the pitch, the other Paint Boys were getting just as annoyed with their number 7. "Wake up!" Danny bellowed from the goal as Leigh let yet another attacker run rings around him. "You morone!" Luke Edwards shouted as Leigh let his curving pass bounce off his left foot and over the line.

Angriest of all, was Gary. Suddenly the offside tactics they'd been practising so successfully all term were not working. There he was, perfectly positioned in the opposition half, waiting for a pass that never came. Time after time, Leigh either lost possession of the ball or kicked it so wildly that Gary couldn't get near it.

"What is the matter with you?" he yelled furiously, as the ball sailed over his head and out of play for the third time. "You're playing like a complete div!"

Leigh winced, but made no reply. Craig saw him glance up into the crowd of spectators. His face was pale. His eyes looked frightened.

Play continued. The Mickelham Mill forwards were already dominating in midfield. Now, sensing the Paint Boys' disarray, they really took control. It was only a matter of time before Mickelham Mill scored the first goal.

Craig hung his head. He couldn't bear to watch. Suddenly, the crowd roared. Craig looked up in alarm. But it was all right. Danny was standing with the ball in his hands.

"Thank God for that!" said Craig.

He saw Danny roll the ball to Maurice, who passed it to Wesley, who chipped it over to Leigh. This was more like it. Fluid play, confident play, accurate play – until it arrived at Leigh's feet, that is.

There, everything went wrong. Leigh stumbled, he fumbled – he dithered so long that Gary mistimed his run. And when Leigh finally punted the ball up the field, the linesman's flag shot up.

Craig groaned. "Offside!" he muttered. Gary had been in the right place at the wrong time. And all because of Leigh!

The worst of it was, Craig had the nagging feeling that Leigh was ... well, doing it on purpose. Playing football was like riding a bike. When you played as much as they did, every move became automatic. *No one* who could play football could suddenly be that bad – unless they wanted to be.

Once again, Leigh looked up into the crowd. Craig watched him chewing his bottom lip anxiously. He saw him nod. What was going on? Why was he so nervous? And who was he communicating with?

Craig turned and craned his neck round in an attempt to see who it might be. But, apart from Danny's grandfather, there was no one that he recognized in the sea of red and green.

All at once, a deafening cheer went up. Craig spun round. Danny was lying face down in the goal-mouth. Their number 9 was punching the air in triumph. The ball was in the back of the net.

"Oh, no," he groaned.

The inevitable had finally happened. Mickelham Mill had gone one goal up.

Craig watched his team moving back into position for the start of play. They all looked thoroughly fed up.

Just before the whistle blew, he caught Leigh glancing up into the crowd for a third time. His face was twitching as if he was trying not to cry. He covered his mouth with his hand, and stared miserably down at the ground. For a moment, Craig felt sorry for him.

But only for a moment.

As the referee started up the game with a blow of his whistle and Leigh removed his hand, Craig saw how wrong he'd been. He gasped with shock.

Leigh hadn't been about to burst into tears at all. He'd been trying to stifle a smile – a smile which, even now, was tugging at the corners of his mouth. He was *glad* they were one-nil down. It could mean only one thing. For whatever reason, Leigh Parker was trying to throw the game.

Chapter 6

Craig's heart pounded furiously; his head was in turmoil. He had to do something. But what? If his suspicions were right, and Leigh *was* trying to throw the game, then he had to be taken off the pitch at once. The trouble was, unless Mr Talbot had seen the smile for himself, he would never believe Leigh capable of such treachery.

As the match continued, Craig grew more and more frustrated. Time and again, Leigh's sloppy tackling allowed the Mickelham Mill forwards to break through. Time and again, his hopeless passes landed at the feet of the opposition. Once, a wild back-kick almost ended up as an own goal. It was only Danny's quick reactions that stopped St Botolph's going two-nil down.

Craig had seen enough. He slid across the bench to Mr Talbot and asked him outright whether it wasn't time for a substitution. "There's a weakness on the left wing," he said, taking care not to mention Leigh by name. "We've got to get the ball up to the forwards more."

Mr Talbot nodded absent-mindedly. "I hear what you're saying," he said.

Craig, however, was not convinced that Mr Talbot had heard a single word. He slid back to the other end of the bench, feeling more nervous than ever. He'd run out of nails to chew. All round him, the "Varnish" version of Amazing Grace was drowning out the half-hearted cries of "Come on, you Paint Boys."

Five minutes later, the whistle went for the end of the first half. Craig breathed a sigh of relief. Given the way the two teams were playing, it was a miracle that St Botolph's were only one goal down.

The moment the whistle sounded, Mr Talbot hurried on to the pitch with a trayful of quartered oranges and a much needed pep talk. "What the hell do you think you're playing at?" he stormed. "I've seen more life in a sack of cement! This is the final, for Pete's sake. Don't you want to win?"

The boys all hung their heads, and shuffled about awkwardly on the muddy grass.

Mr Talbot breathed in sharply. "Luckily for you, football's a game of two halves. We're down, but we're not beaten." He looked round. "I want you to get out there. Keep your heads. Remember what we've practised. And..." He stopped. "Gary Connell! Leigh Parker! Are you listening to me?"

The short answer was, no. While Mr Talbot was speaking, Gary had leant forwards and whispered "Banana Brain!" into Leigh's ear. Leigh had responded with "You and whose army?" Gary had shoved him, and Leigh punched him back. Neither of them were now aware that Mr Talbot had turned his attention on them.

"You're not even trying!" Gary shouted.

"Oh, yeah!" Leigh shouted back. "Is it my fault you keep losing the ball?"

"Yes!" Gary yelled. "Yes, it is. You haven't given me a decent pass all match. I reckon Craig was right. You—"

Mr Talbot strode angrily towards the two boys and seized them firmly by the shoulders. "Will you two stop this, right now!" he said, his voice hard and cold. "Or I'll take you both off. Understood?"

Gary immediately fell silent. Leigh, on the other hand – and much to Craig's surprise – seemed devastated.

"No," he said, his voice quavering. "You can't. You mustn't. I've got to play on..."

Mr Talbot stared at the boy curiously. "Yes, well," he said finally. "Just pull your socks up. If you're going to win this game, you've got to work together as a team. All right?"

"Yes, sir," said Leigh meekly. "Thank you."

The second half started better for St Botolph's. They were much tighter in the midfield and had more possession of the ball. The equalizer, however, remained elusive. It was thanks to

Wesley Hunter's quick thinking in the sixty-eighth minute that this changed.

With their number 3 rocketing towards him with the ball, Wesley ran in hard and tackled the ball away. Then, without a pause, he kicked it on to Luke Edwards on the right wing. Luke dummied a cross, and continued on towards the goal.

Mickelham Mill were in sudden confusion. They were used to attacks from the left, not the right.

Finding himself unchallenged, Luke carried on with the ball and took a shot from just outside the penalty box. The ball flew like an arrow, beating the goalie, and crashed into the far corner of the net.

"YEAH!" Craig bellowed. They'd done it. They'd equalized. "Come on, you Paint Boys!" he cried out. "Come on, you Paint Boys!"

As other St Botolph's supporters in

the crowd took up the chant, Craig himself fell silent. He stared at Leigh in disbelief. While the rest of the team were leaping about gleefully, Leigh himself looked crestfallen. Once more, Craig saw him glancing up into the mass of spectators. This time, however, he turned away again almost immediately. The look on his face was one of terror.

With only twenty minutes left, and everything to play for, the match suddenly became fast and furious. First Mickelham Mill had a shot at goal, which Danny saved. Then the game speeded up to the other end of the pitch, with Luke Edwards trying – unsuccessfully – for a goal. Then back again. Both teams scented victory, but it was still anyone's guess which way the match would go.

Suddenly, their number 4 intercepted a pass meant for Luke Edwards, and started a run for goal. Craig sat forward in his seat and gnawed at his knuckles. Danny darted about from one side to the other, trying to keep his eye on the ball.

Wesley Hunter raced towards the number 4, but was left standing as the ball was chipped past him. Craig groaned.

But it was all right. Although he'd beaten Wesley, the attacker now had to face Maurice Meacham and Ricky Baker. He'd never get past them both. And since no one had run with him, he couldn't pass the ball. Craig was feeling confident the danger was over when, all at once, he noticed Leigh Parker abandon his position on the left wing and hurtle towards their number 4 like a maniac.

At least he's actually *doing* something for once, Craig thought. The next instant, however, his relief turned to horror.

Distracted by Leigh's sudden arrival on the scene, both Maurice and Ricky made a fatal hesitation. The number 4 slipped between them, and on towards the goal. Danny ran forward to crowd him out as best he could. The attacker moved into the penalty box.

Craig gasped and hugged his knees tightly to his chest. He looked at their number 4. He looked at Danny. He looked at Leigh, racing towards the pair of them.

Then, without any warning, Leigh launched himself at the Mickelham Mill player, feet first and studs exposed. He crashed against the boy's left shin with a sickening crunch. The boy screamed with pain, and fell writhing to the ground.

The referee blew his whistle furiously.

The Mickelham Mill supporters began chanting "Off! Off! Off! Off!"

The referee agreed with them. He showed Leigh the red card, took his name and sent him off angrily. "And if it was up to me, you'd never play in another Junior League match again," Craig heard him shouting.

Leigh walked from the pitch, head down, shamefaced and to the accompaniment of loud booing. Two men passed him. They were carrying a stretcher.

Craig was in despair. He felt sorry for their number 4. Of course he did. Leigh's behaviour was unforgivable.

But – and it was a big but – he also felt sorry for his own team. Not only were the Paint Boys down to ten men, but they were also facing a penalty. Things could hardly be worse.

Chapter 7

Mr Talbot was so angry that he could hardly speak. He glared at Leigh, white-faced and tight-lipped, as the boy approached him.

"I'm ashamed of you, Leigh," he said. "Ashamed."

Leigh nodded, but made no attempt either to apologize or to explain.

"Go on," said Mr Talbot icily, his top lip curling. "Go and get changed. We'll speak about it later."

Leigh turned and walked away. As he passed the subs' bench, Craig leapt to his feet and grabbed him by the shirt.

"What on earth did you do that for?" he demanded.

"What? What?" said Leigh innocently.

Craig released him and turned away in disgust. "You're not worth it," he muttered.

Leigh shrugged and walked off – glancing up into the crowd one last time as he went.

Craig sat down again and looked at Danny sympathetically. He had played in goal occasionally. He knew just what was going on in Danny's mind as the Mickelham Mill number 10 placed the ball on the penalty spot.

The referee blew the whistle. The penalty could now go ahead. Danny positioned himself just to the left of centre in goal, and waited.

There is only one way to save a penalty – unless the striker makes a complete mess of it – and that is to commit yourself to the direction you are going to leap. Left or right, you have to decide which way to go *before* the ball is struck. Afterwards, it's too late. By standing slightly to the left, Danny was trying to make the striker aim for the right. That was the way he was going to jump.

The boy stepped back, counting out the paces. Danny swayed from left to right. The boy glanced up. There was revenge in his eyes. Suddenly, he was running – one, two, three – and WHAM!

The ball flew. Arms outstretched, Danny leapt to the right. The ball landed in the back of the net – to his left. He had paid the price for being outbluffed.

Things *had* got worse after all, Craig realized miserably. Not only were they playing with ten men, not only were they weak on the left wing, but now they were also two-one down. Apart from some injury time, there were only twelve minutes to go until the final whistle. It was looking more and more unlikely that St Botolph's would make that all-important double.

Craig looked along the bench. If Mr Talbot took off Wesley Hunter, who was playing in midfield, and put him on instead, he could cover the centre *and* left of the pitch. After all, unlike all the others, Craig still had loads of energy. But Mr Talbot seemed distracted.

"Never seen anything like it," he was muttering unhappily. "Not from one of my boys."

Sensing imminent victory, the Mickelham Mill spectators were going wild. They were whooping and whistling, cheering and chanting. As Craig looked round at their faces, gleeful with anticipation, he felt worse than ever. He was about to turn back when all at once, his gaze focused on someone he did recognize – a boy of about fifteen or sixteen.

Before, when Craig had looked into the crowd, the boy must have been wearing his baseball cap. Now he was waving it triumphantly in the air. The bright afternoon sunshine glinted on his shaved head. It was Leigh's cousin, whistling and cheering with the rest.

But why? Leigh had been sent off, and now his team were two-one down. So, how come Billy looked so happy? Craig knew it must have something to do with the conversation he'd overheard in the changing cubicle. They'd talked about the football final then. And an agreement. And the roller-blades. And Leigh's mother. "This means a lot to me," Billy had said. Craig was more convinced than ever that Leigh had been trying to throw the game. But the question remained. Why? Somehow, he had to find out.

Without knowing what he was going to say when he got there, he set off in the direction of cousin Billy. He pushed and shoved his way blindly through the huge crowd. Closer and closer he got. Billy came back into view. Craig stared at him – and stopped.

He gasped. Now he understood everything. Before he had a chance to decide what to do next, however, he heard Mr Talbot calling for him. "Craig? Craig Taggart, where are you lad?"

Craig dashed back down to the side of the pitch. "Here, sir," he said.

Mr Talbot nodded. "You're on," he said.

Chapter 8

Without a second thought, Craig bounded on to the pitch. It was – just as he had predicted – Wesley who was coming off. Craig raised the palm of his hand and, as they passed one another, Wesley slapped it.

"Good luck, mate," he said.

They were in a tight corner. In fact, two-one down, eleven players versus ten and, with little more than ten minutes till the end of the match, corners didn't get much tighter. Yet Craig felt good.

"All right?" he called out cheerily to

Gary and Danny. It was just like old times.

The game soon became faster and more furious than ever – despite Mickelham Mill's efforts to slow the game down. With Craig on the pitch, it was as though everyone else on the team had suddenly been revitalized. What was more, for the first time since the match had started, all their after-school practice was finally starting to pay off.

Finding himself in possession of the ball, Craig ran forward two paces and kicked it up the field. Gary, who had drawn his marker forward, sprinted off to where the ball was already coming in to land.

Gary trapped it expertly at his feet, flicked it round and advanced towards the goal.

"Go on, Gary!" Craig roared encouragingly.

The goalie – determined not to make the same mistake twice – rushed forwards. But the Paint Boys had practised for this with Mr Talbot, too. Luke Edwards was already racing towards the goal, taking care to stay onside.

"Cross it to me!" he yelled. "Now!"

Gary steadied up and chipped the ball delicately into the air. He couldn't have positioned it better. Luke leapt up and headed it. The ball whistled past the goalie and into the net.

It was two-all!

The St Botolph supporters suddenly refound their voices – and how! A deafening chorus of "Come on, you Paint Boys!" echoed round the pitch in waves. In contrast, the Paint Boys themselves remained quiet. There would be time to celebrate when they won – *if* they won.

As they lined up for the kick-off,

Craig glanced round into the crowd. Cousin Billy looked furious. He was shaking his fist angrily at the ref, and bellowing "OFFSIDE!"

Craig smirked. "We'll show you," he muttered.

Mickelham Mill kicked off quickly. No longer ahead, they were now as desperate to score as St Botolph's. This way and that, the ball was kicked. Up and down the pitch. Throw-ins were taken fast, goal-kicks were punted as far into the opposition half as possible. The game was becoming increasingly frantic – and dirty – as the twenty-one remaining players gave it their all to make sure their team would win the cup.

A free kick was awarded to St Botolph's when Ricky Baker was brought down by a particularly vicious sliding tackle. Maurice Meacham took the ball, and chipped it over to Craig who, realizing that he was on his own, made a run for goal.

He fought off two challenges, and was just about to pass it up to Gary when he noticed his marker had left him. Gary was offside. Craig had no choice but to go it alone.

On he ran, the ball seemingly glued to his feet, past a defender and on over the penalty line. Opposition players were streaking towards him. The crowd was roaring. At the last possible moment, he took a shot at goal.

The kick was a beaut! It sliced through the air, rising all the time. It was still rising as it clipped the goalie's outstretched fingertips – and *still* rising as it slammed into the back of the net. The referee blew his whistle for a goal.

Craig clenched his fists in victory and fell to his knees. He'd proved himself. "Yes!" he shouted. "YES!"

The St Botolph supporters went

crazy, screaming and shouting, and jumping up and down with their red scarves flapping above their heads. The referee blew his whistle a second time – a long two-tone blast.

The game was over and St Botolph's had done it! They'd won the Mereside Borough Junior Cup for two years running.

Gary, Luke and Craig – the three goal-scorers – were hoisted up on to the shoulders of their team-mates and paraded round the pitch. "We are the Paint Boys! We are the Paint Boys!" they all chanted.

From his vantage point, high up in the air, Craig saw cousin Billy toss away his baseball cap in disgust and march off. He noted where it fell and, when the others finally placed him back down on the ground, ran over to retrieve it.

It was green – the same shade as the

Mickelham Mill strip. Craig picked it up and turned it over in his hand. And there, at the front and stitched with yellow thread, were the two words he had noticed earlier.

Varley's Varnish.

Chapter 9

The atmosphere in the changing room was electric. Everyone was talking at once after their three-two victory.

"What about the way Maurice tackled their number 7!" "Yeah, and did you see Ricky's pass – just after he was fouled that first time." "And Luke's header!" "The goalie never stood a chance. And then *Craig's* goal." "Brilliant!" "Inspired!" "Magic!"

On and on they went, babbling happily to one another – reliving the goals and recounting the bits of the game that would stick in their memories for ever. Only one person was not contributing to the general hubbub. Leigh Parker. Up at the far end of the changing room, he was sitting on his own.

If the team had lost, or even drawn, then the other players would definitely have been giving Leigh a hard time. But they hadn't lost or drawn. They'd won. For the second year running, they'd won the cup, and Leigh Parker was an irrelevance. The others ignored him completely.

Only Craig wondered why Leigh was hanging about. After all, he'd been sent in for an early shower, yet he still wasn't dressed. Perhaps he was too ashamed to go home after what he'd done. Or perhaps he was frightened cousin Billy was out there waiting for him. Although Craig thought he knew, now, why Leigh had thrown the game, questions still remained – questions

Craig was determined to get answers to.

In rowdy twos and threes the team gradually set off for home. When they were ready, Gary and Danny called out for Craig.

"Are you coming?"

"In a minute," Craig said. "I just want to ... to check if that shin-pad's turned up in the lost property box."

"We'll wait," said Danny.

"No, you go on," said Craig. "I'll catch you up."

Gary nodded towards the far end of the changing room. "Sure you want to stay?" he said. "There's a horrible smell in here."

Craig smiled. "I won't be long," he said.

With Danny and Gary finally gone, only two boys remained in the changing room.

Craig walked across to where Leigh

was standing, back turned. "Happy we won the cup, then, are you?" he said.

"Yeah. Course I am," said Leigh, as he continued to stuff his kit into his sports bag.

Craig stared at Leigh's back. He could feel himself getting angrier and angrier. "Liar!" he said.

Leigh spun round. "You what?" he demanded.

"You heard," said Craig.

Leigh dumped his bag on the floor, took a step forwards and shoved Craig hard in the chest. "No one calls me a liar," he said, and shoved him a second time.

Craig staggered backwards, ashen-faced with fury. He squared up and stared defiantly into Leigh's face, "Liar!" he repeated, coldly, quietly.

Leigh lunged forwards at him. But Craig was ready for him. He dodged to one side and punched him hard in the stomach with his left fist. Winded, Leigh doubled over. Craig struck him in the face with his right.

"Admit it!" he yelled. "Admit you were trying to throw the game."

But Leigh had no intention of admitting anything. Head down, he threw himself at Craig, and the pair of them fell noisily to the floor. Finding himself lying underneath the heavier boy, Craig brought his knee up sharply. Leigh groaned and rolled away. Craig climbed to his feet.

"Admit it!" he said again. "You wanted us to lose. Playing like a div. And that foul!"

Leigh climbed groggily to his feet. But Craig wasn't finished yet. He leapt forwards and caught him in a headlock.

"You gave away that penalty on purpose," he said.

"I ... I..." Leigh grunted, as he wriggled and writhed and twisted around. Suddenly, his left elbow slammed into Craig's stomach. Craig gasped and tottered backwards. Leigh leapt at him, shoved him back to the ground and pinned him face down.

"He was going to score," he panted. "There was nothing else I could do. You've gotta believe me."

Craig snorted. "Liar!" he said, and began thrashing about furiously. "Liar! Liar! Liar!"

He freed his right arm, reached up, seized Leigh around the back of his neck and pulled it down sharply. He felt – and heard – Leigh's nose cracking into the back of his head. Leigh instantly released his grip. Craig quickly rolled over, slammed Leigh back on to the floor and seized him by the front of his jacket.

"Now will you admit that you were trying to throw the game!" he bellowed.

Leigh dabbed at his bleeding nose with the back of his hand. His face was blotchy red; his eyes were welling with tears. "You're a nutter, you are, Craig Taggart!" he sniffed.

Craig said nothing. He could wait.

"I... Anyone can have an off-day," Leigh went on. "Throwing the game! You're just jealous 'cos I'm in the team and you're not. Throwing the game!" he said again. "Where's your proof."

Craig abruptly released his grip on Leigh's jacket. Leigh's head dropped back to the wooden floor with a bang. Without saying a word, Craig stood up. He walked over to his bag. Reached inside. Pulled something out and tossed it down at Leigh's feet.

"You want proof," he said calmly. "There's your proof." The pair of them stared down at the green baseball cap with the yellow stitching. "It's your cousin Billy's," said Craig.

The colour drained from Leigh's face. He picked up the baseball cap and climbed unsteadily to his feet. "I ... I ... didn't know he was watching the match," he said.

"Liar," said Craig again. "I saw you looking at him. Nodding. Smiling... And then I got to thinking about that conversation the two of you had in the swimming-baths. Do you remember? About the final with Mickleham Mill. About the roller-blades, the elbow guards, the knee pads... Do you want to know what I reckon!" he said. "I reckon your cousin Billy bribed you to throw the game. With the blades and all the protective gear. That's why you were playing so badly. That's why you gave away that penalty – why you smacked into that poor bloke's leg like that."

Leigh swallowed. "Do you think it's broken?" he said.

"No thanks to you if it isn't," said Craig. "And it'd serve you right if you broke *your* leg when you're out on your ... your *Judas* roller-blades."

Leigh sighed. He pulled a wad of

tissues from his pocket, wiped away the blood from his nose and looked up at Craig. "He isn't my real cousin," he said miserably. "He used to go out with my sister."

Craig was shocked. "But he looked horrible!" he said.

"He is," said Leigh.

Craig remained stony-faced. "And his name wouldn't happen to be Billy *Varley*, would it?" he said.

Leigh nodded. "His father owns Varley's Varnish. They reckoned that if the team they were sponsoring won, they'd get thousands of pounds of free advertizing. Scupper Pringle's Paints once and for all." He shrugged. "I don't know whose idea it was – Billy's or his dad's. They're both as rotten as each other."

"It wouldn't have worked if you hadn't gone along with it," Craig reminded him. "Blimey!" he said. "To think that you'd have sacrificed the Junior Cup for a pair of roller-blades." He shook his head in disbelief. "It's…"

"N-n-no," Leigh interrupted. He was close to tears. "That wasn't how it was."

"Then why did you try and throw the match?" Craig persisted.

Leigh looked down at the ground. He wiped his eyes on his sleeve. He sniffed.

"Mum bought me the roller-blades for Christmas," he began. "But she couldn't afford all the guards and that. So Billy takes me into town. Tells me he knows this place where they do fantastic bargains. Ac-tion-e, it's called."

Craig whistled. Ac-tion-e was notoriously expensive.

Leigh went on. "So, anyway," he said. "Billy selects these three pairs of guards. Forty-two pounds a throw it says on the label, but Billy promises me they're on special offer. "A *very* special offer!" he said. It was only when he suddenly stuffs them inside my bomber jacket and drags me from the shop that I realize what he means. And by then it was too late."

"You mean, you nicked them?" said Craig.

Leigh nodded. "It all happened so fast," he said. "One minute we were standing looking round. The next minute we're being chased down the High Street by two big blokes from the shop. It was awful."

"But you got away," said Craig.

"Yeah," said Leigh glumly. "We got away." He sighed. "Then Billy explained all about the football competition. Said it was important for him that the team they were sponsoring – Mickelham Mill – won the cup." He paused, and when he spoke again, his voice was shaky. "He ... he said that if we beat them, then he'd tell my mum that I'd been shoplifting."

Craig frowned with concern. "So he *was* blackmailing you."

Leigh nodded miserably. His lower lip was trembling again. "I was frightened," he said. "You don't know what a temper he's got on him."

"I think I can guess," said Craig. Billy Varley would have intimidated anybody, and Craig began to wonder just how Mickelham Mill had made it to the final in the first place. How many other games had Billy Varley nobbled to make sure that Varley's Varnish had sponsored the winning team?

"Do you know the funny thing?" Leigh went on.

"What's that?" said Craig.

Leigh smiled weakly. "I haven't even dared to use the stuff we took. It's all still in the original packaging."

Craig stared back at Leigh. He didn't know what to do or say. Suddenly, he felt very young. This was a problem for grown-ups to sort out – Leigh's mum or Mr Talbot, or perhaps even the police. He stepped forwards and patted Leigh clumsily on the shoulder.

"It'll be all right," he said.

Leigh looked up. "I *am* glad we ... you won," he said. "I don't think I could have lived with myself if..."

"Yeah, well," said Craig awkwardly. "It was just as well I was there in the swimming-baths that morning. Otherwise things might have turned out very different."

Leigh smiled. "You were in the right place at the right time, I guess," he said.

"*On*side!" they said together, and burst out laughing.

Chapter 10

The following afternoon, Gary and Danny were surprised to see Craig setting off with Leigh in the direction of town.

"Where are you going, Craig?" Gary called.

"Got some unfinished business to sort out," Craig called back. "I'll catch you up the rec later."

"Yeah, but you needn't bring your friend," Gary shouted back.

Craig and Leigh ignored him. There would be time for explanations later on. They continued along the pavement in silence. The centre of town got closer. Leigh was dragging his feet. At the clock tower they turned left. The illuminated green Ac-tion-e sign flashed at them from the opposite side of the road.

Leigh stopped. "I can't," he said.

"You've got to," said Craig, pulling him by the arm. "Come on."

They crossed the road, Leigh took a deep breath, and the pair of them entered the shop.

"Can I help you, lads?" said the shopkeeper.

"It's... I've..." Leigh began. He gulped, reached into his pockets and put the three packs of guards and pads down on the counter. "I'm bringing these back," he said.

"I'll need a receipt if you want to change them," said the man.

"I haven't got a receipt," Leigh said, and told him everything that had happened. As the story unfolded, the man's face turned from surprise to anger to concern – and back to surprise.

"And so you brought them back," he said. He took a deep breath. "I could still prosecute, you know," he said. "Shoplifting is shoplifting..."

Leigh shrugged unhappily.

"But... Under the circumstances... And seeing as you have returned the items. Untouched..." He shook his head. "It's a shame we can't get this Billy Varley character, though."

Craig nodded. He, too, hated the idea of Billy getting off scot-free. It was so unfair.

"The trouble is," the shopkeeper went on, "if I let you off, I'll have to let him off, too."

"But if Leigh told the police what really happened," said Craig.

"I already thought of that," said

Leigh. "It would just be my word against his."

"Better all round if we let the matter drop, I think," said the shopkeeper. "Anyway," he added. "Type like that, he's bound to get caught for something else sooner or later." He looked up and winked. "Go on, then, the pair of you. Clear off!"

Neither Craig nor Leigh needed telling twice. With a final "Thanks again!" they made for the door.

"He was all right, wasn't he?" said Leigh, when they were out of earshot.

"Yeah," said Craig. "Nice bloke. He was right though, it *is* a shame that Billy's been let off. I..." He stopped, and grabbed Leigh's arm.

"What? What is it?" said Leigh.

"Looks like it's happened sooner rather than later," said Craig.

"What has?" said Leigh.

Craig pointed at the pile of newspapers stacked up in the window of the newsagent's. "Recognize someone?" he said.

Leigh peered in through the glass. His jaw dropped. "I don't believe it," he said.

There, splashed across the front page of the *Mereside Evening Courier* was the headline, VARLEY VARNISH SON ARRESTED. Below it was a large photo of Billy Varley himself being led from a doorway in handcuffs by two police constables.

Leigh dashed into the shop, picked up a newspaper and began reading. Craig peered over his shoulder. The news was disappointingly sketchy. Apparently, Billy had been arrested the previous evening after police had been called to "a disturbance" at the local off-licence.

"My sister, Sharon, used to go out

with him," came a voice, behind them.

They looked round. It was Tracy, with Toyah at her side. Craig turned to Leigh. "Seems like everyone's sister's gone out with him," he said.

But Leigh wasn't listening. "Did you like him?" he asked Tracy.

"What, Billy Varley? No. He was horrible," she said, and added. "It's not the first time he's smashed up an offy."

"He smashed it up!" Leigh exclaimed.

"Goes berserk if anyone asks him for ID," said Tracy.

"Wild," said Toyah.

"Last time they put him on probation," Tracy went on. "This time they reckon he'll get sent down."

"Bound to," said Toyah.

"And good riddance," said Tracy. "Anyway," she said a moment later, "catch you both later. Come on, Toy."

And with that, the pair of them were gone.

Leigh looked at Craig, then back down at the newspaper. A smile spread over his face. "I bet this wasn't what he had in mind when he was talking about free advertizing!" he said.

Craig laughed. "See," he said. "I told you everything would be all right."

" 'Ere!" came a voice from behind them. "Are you gonna buy that paper, or what?"

"Yes," said Leigh. "In fact, I'm going to buy eleven of them."

He had decided that everyone on the team deserved an explanation for his behaviour. It would be ten times harder even than returning the pads and guards to Ac-tion-e. But he had no choice. It was the least he could do.

Gary and Danny were far from pleased to see that Leigh was still

with Craig when he arrived at the rec.

"I thought I told you not to bring your friend," Gary said, deliberately avoiding Leigh's gaze.

"Leigh's got something to say," said Craig.

"Yeah, well, what if I don't want to listen?" said Gary.

"I think you should," said Craig, staring him out. He turned to Leigh. "Go on, then. Tell them."

And Leigh did tell them. He told them everything – the whole sorry story. He gave them each a copy of the newspaper so that they could see for themselves the type of person he had been up against. And when they had finished reading, he said one last thing.

"I'm sorry." He hung his head. "Really sorry."

Finally it was over.

Danny stepped forward and put his

hand on Leigh's arm. "There's something I wasn't going to tell you," he said.

"What?" said Leigh, worried about what was going to come next.

"That kid you fouled," said Danny. "His leg isn't broken. Just badly bruised."

"How do you know?" said Leigh.

"His grandma knows my grandad," said Danny.

Leigh sighed with relief. "Thank God for that," he said.

Danny laughed. "I wouldn't get *too* happy about it," he said. "Apparently he's promised to get you the moment he's up and about."

"Has he, now?" said Gary. "We'll have to see about that. Come on, then, you lot," he shouted as he trotted off. "Let's play two aside, with rush-goalies. Me and Leigh against you two. OK?"

"OK!" the others shouted back.

The sun had set and the light was fading fast by the time the four friends collected up their sweatshirts and set off for home. And, as they crossed the football pitch towards the park gates, they linked arms and burst into song.

"We won the cup. We won the cup. E-i-adio, we won the cup!"

"It's a pity we're going up to the senior school at the end of the year," Leigh said. "Otherwise we could have gone for the hat trick."

Gary laughed. "Didn't you know?" he said. "The cup's open to anyone under twelve. We've got one more year."

"Hat trick, here we come!" Danny yelled, and they all started chanting.

"'Ere we go, 'ere we go, 'ere we go. 'Ere we go, 'ere we go, 'ere we go-o!"